The Premature Burial

By

Edgar A. Poe

(published 1850)

British Library Cataloguing-in-Publication Data
A catalogue record for this book is available from the
British Library

Edgar Allan Poe

Edgar Allan Poe was born in Boston, Massachusetts, on 19th January, 1809.

Best known for his tales of mystery and the macabre, Poe was one of the earliest American practitioners of the short story, and is generally considered the inventor of the 'detective fiction' genre.

Edgar Allan Poe was the second child of English-born actress Elizabeth Arnold Hopkins Poe, and actor David Poe, Jr. He was left an orphan at a very young age however, following the abscondence of his father (in 1810) and the subsequent death of his mother (1811). After this early tragedy, Poe was taken into the home of John Allan, a successful Scottish merchant in Richmond, Virginia, who dealt in a variety of goods including tobacco, cloth, wheat, tombstones, and slaves. The Allans served as a foster family and gave him the name 'Edgar Allan Poe', though they never formally adopted him.

After a brief spell living in England and Scotland (where he attended a grammar school in Irvine, Scotland, and a boarding school in Chelsea, London), Poe moved back with the Allans to Richmond, Virginia, in 1820. In March 1825, John Allan's uncle and business benefactor William Galt, said to be one of the wealthiest men in Richmond, died and left Allan several acres of real estate. The inheritance was estimated at $750,000. By summer 1825, Allan celebrated his expansive wealth by purchasing a two-story brick home named 'Moldavia'.

Edgar Allan Poe may have become engaged to Sarah Elmira Royster before he registered at the one-year-old University of Virginia in February 1826 – to study ancient and modern languages. During his time there, Poe lost touch with Royster and also became estranged from his foster father over gambling debts. Poe claimed that Allan had not given him sufficient money to register for classes, purchase texts, and procure and furnish a dormitory. Allan did send additional money and clothes, but Poe's debts increased.

Edgar Allan Poe gave up on the university after a year, and, not feeling welcome in Richmond, especially when he learned that his sweetheart Royster had married Alexander Shelton, he travelled to Boston in April 1827, sustaining himself with odd jobs as a clerk and newspaper writer. By now in severe financial trouble, Poe lied about his age in order to enlist in the army. It was around this time that Poe started writing.

In 1827 he released his first book, a forty-page collection of poetry, *Tamerlane and Other Poems*, attributed with the byline 'by a Bostonian'. Only fifty copies were printed, and the book received virtually no attention. Whilst in the army, Poe also wrote satirical poems and verses about his commanding officers. After spending two years posted to South Carolina, and having failed as an officer's cadet at West Point, Poe left the military by deliberately getting court-martialled.

Edgar Allan Poe left for New York in 1831, where he

released his third collection of poems, the first two having received almost zero attention. Not long after its publication, in March of 1831, Poe returned to Baltimore. After his early attempts at poetry, Poe had turned his attention to prose. He placed a few stories with a Philadelphia publication and began work on his only drama, *Politian*. The *Baltimore Saturday Visiter* awarded Poe a prize in October 1833 for his short story 'MS. Found in a Bottle'. The story brought him to the attention of John P. Kennedy, a Baltimorean of considerable means. He helped Poe place some of his stories, and introduced him to Thomas W. White, editor of the *Southern Literary Messenger* in Richmond.

Despite often finding himself penniless, and frequently having to move city find employment, during the thirties and forties Poe published a good amount of fiction. Most of his best known short-stories, such as 'The Black Cat', 'The Pit and the Pendulum', 'The Premature Burial', 'The Tell Tale Heart,' 'Ligeia', 'William Wilson' and 'The Fall of the House of Usher', were published between 1835 and 1845. In January 1845, Poe published his poem 'The Raven', which – despite fact that he only received $9 for it – was a great success, turning him overnight into something of a household name.

In 1835, Edgar Allan Poe (aged twenty-six at the time) married his thirteen year old cousin – Virginia. They appeared to have a happy marriage, but one evening in January 1842, Virginia showed the first signs of consumption. Poe began to drink heavily under the stress of Virginia's illness, and returned to New York, where he worked briefly at the *Evening Mirror* before becoming editor of the *Broadway Journal* and, later, sole owner. There he alienated himself from other writers by publicly accusing Henry Wadsworth Longfellow of plagiarism, though Longfellow never responded. Virginia died in 1847.

'Annabel Lee' was Edgar Allan Poe's last complete poem (written in 1849) – exploring the theme of the death of a beautiful woman. The narrator, who fell in love with Annabel Lee when they were young, has a love for her so strong that even angels are envious – retaining his love even after her death. There has been much debate over who, if anyone, was the inspiration for 'Annabel Lee', but Virginia has been postulated as the most likely candidate.

Edgar Allan Poe himself died two years later, on 7th October 1849, aged just forty. Rather fittingly for such a master of the macabre, the circumstances were somewhat odd. He was found wandering the streets of Baltimore at five in the morning, delirious and wearing someone else's clothes, and he repeatedly cried out 'Reynolds!' during the hours before his death. His final words were reportedly, 'Lord help my poor soul.' The cause of death remains a mystery, as all medical records, including his death certificate have been lost. Everything from epilepsy to rabies, has been cited as a possible cause.

Whatever the reason behind his unusual passing, Edgar Allan Poe's legacy is a formidable one. He is seen today as one of the greatest practitioners of Gothic and detective fiction that ever lived, and popular culture is replete with references to him. Poe's work also greatly influenced science fiction, notably Jules Verne, who wrote a sequel to Poe's novel *The Narrative of Arthur Gordon Pym of Nantucket* called *An Antarctic Mystery*, also known as *The Sphinx of the Ice Fields*.

Even so, Poe has received not only praise, but criticism as well. This is partly because of the negative perception of his personal character and its influence upon his reputation. William Butler Yeats was occasionally critical of Poe and once called him 'vulgar'. Transcendentalist Ralph Waldo Emerson reacted to 'The Raven' by saying, 'I see nothing in it', and Aldous Huxley wrote that Poe's writing 'falls into vulgarity' by being 'too poetical – the equivalent of wearing a diamond ring on every finger.'

Despite this, Edgar Allan Poe's work has seen a massive upsurge in popularity in the present day – appreciated all over the globe, and translated into many different languages. He is as much loved for his poignant poetry as for his scintillating short stories, and his influence continues to be felt.

The Premature Burial

THERE are certain themes of which the interest is all-absorbing, but which are too entirely horrible for the purposes of legitimate fiction. These the mere romanticist must eschew, if he do not wish to offend or to disgust. They are with propriety handled only when the severity and majesty of Truth sanctify and sustain them. We thrill, for example, with the most intense of "pleasurable pain" over the accounts of the Passage of the Beresina, of the Earthquake at Lisbon, of the Plague at London, of the Massacre of St. Bartholomew, or of the stifling of the hundred and twenty-three prisoners in the Black Hole at Calcutta. But in these accounts it is the fact -- it is the reality -- it is the history which excites. As inventions, we should regard them with simple abhorrence.

I have mentioned some few of the more prominent and august calamities on record; but in these it is the extent, not less than the character of the calamity, which so vividly impresses the fancy. I need not remind the reader that, from the long and weird catalogue of human miseries, I might have selected many individual instances more replete with essential suffering than any of these vast generalities of disaster. The true wretchedness, indeed -- the ultimate woe -- is particular, not diffuse. That the ghastly extremes of agony are endured by man the unit, and never by man the mass -- for this let us thank a merciful God!

To be buried while alive is, beyond question, the most terrific of these extremes which has ever fallen to the lot of mere mortality. That it has frequently, very frequently, so fallen will scarcely be denied by those who think. The boundaries which divide Life from Death are at best shadowy and vague. Who shall say where the one ends, and where the other begins? We know that there are diseases in which occur total cessations of all the apparent functions of vitality, and yet in which these cessations are merely suspensions, properly so called. They are only temporary pauses in the incomprehensible mechanism. A certain period elapses, and some unseen mysterious principle again sets in motion the magic pinions and the wizard wheels. The silver cord was not for ever loosed, nor the golden bowl irreparably broken. But where, meantime, was the soul?

Apart, however, from the inevitable conclusion, a priori that such causes must produce such effects --that the well-known occurrence of such cases of suspended animation must naturally give rise, now and then, to premature interments --apart from this consideration, we have the direct testimony of medical and ordinary experience to prove that a vast number of such interments have actually taken place. I might refer at once, if necessary to a hundred well authenticated instances. One of very remarkable character, and of which the circumstances may be fresh in the memory of some of my readers, occurred, not very long ago, in the neighboring city of Baltimore, where it occasioned a painful, intense, and widely-extended excitement. The wife of one of the most respectable citizens-a lawyer of eminence and a member of Congress --was seized with a sudden and unaccountable illness, which completely baffled the skill of her physicians. After much suffering she died, or was supposed to die. No one suspected, indeed, or had reason to suspect, that she was not actually dead. She presented all the ordinary appearances of death. The face assumed the usual pinched and sunken outline. The lips were of the usual marble pallor. The eyes were lustreless. There was no warmth. Pulsation had ceased. For three days the body was preserved unburied, during which it had acquired a stony rigidity. The funeral, in short, was hastened, on account of the rapid advance of what was supposed to be decomposition.

The lady was deposited in her family vault, which, for three subsequent years, was undisturbed. At the expiration of this term it was opened for the reception of a sarcophagus; -- but, alas! how fearful a shock awaited the husband, who, personally, threw open the door! As its portals swung outwardly back, some white-apparelled object fell rattling within his arms. It was the skeleton of his wife in her yet unmoulded shroud.

A careful investigation rendered it evident that she had revived within two days after her entombment; that her struggles within the coffin had caused it to fall from a ledge, or shelf to the floor, where it was so broken as to permit her escape. A lamp which had been accidentally left, full of oil, within the tomb, was found empty; it might have been exhausted, however, by evaporation. On the uttermost of the steps which led down into the dread chamber was a large fragment of the coffin, with which, it seemed, that she had endeavored to arrest attention by striking the iron door. While thus occupied, she probably swooned, or possibly died, through sheer terror; and, in failing, her shroud became entangled in some iron -- work which projected interiorly. Thus she remained, and thus she rotted, erect.

In the year 1810, a case of living inhumation happened in France, attended with circumstances which go far to warrant the assertion that truth is, indeed, stranger than fiction. The heroine of the story was a Mademoiselle Victorine Lafourcade, a young girl of illustrious family, of wealth, and of great personal beauty. Among her numerous suitors was Julien Bossuet, a poor litterateur, or journalist of Paris. His talents and general amiability had recommended him to the notice of the heiress, by whom he seems to have been truly beloved; but her pride of birth decided her, finally, to reject him, and to wed a Monsieur Renelle, a banker and a diplomatist of some eminence. After marriage, however, this gentleman neglected, and, perhaps, even more positively ill-treated her. Having passed with him some wretched years, she died, -- at least her condition so closely resembled death as to deceive every one who saw her. She was buried -- not in a vault, but in an ordinary grave in the village of her nativity. Filled with despair, and still inflamed by the memory of a profound attachment, the lover journeys from the capital to the remote province in which the village lies, with the romantic purpose of disinterring the corpse, and possessing himself of its luxuriant tresses. He reaches the grave. At midnight he unearths the coffin, opens it, and is in the act of detaching the hair, when he is arrested by the unclosing of the beloved eyes. In fact, the lady had been buried alive. Vitality had not altogether departed, and she was aroused by the caresses of her lover from the lethargy which had been mistaken for death. He bore her frantically to his lodgings in the village. He employed certain powerful restoratives suggested by no little medical learning. In fine, she revived. She recognized her preserver. She remained with him until, by slow degrees, she fully recovered her original health. Her woman's heart was not adamant, and this last lesson of love sufficed to soften it. She bestowed it upon Bossuet. She returned no more to her husband, but, concealing from him her resurrection, fled with her lover to America. Twenty years afterward, the two returned to France, in the persuasion that time had so greatly altered the lady's appearance that her friends would be unable to recognize her. They were mistaken, however, for, at the first meeting, Monsieur Renelle did actually recognize and make claim to his wife. This claim she resisted, and a judicial tribunal sustained her in her resistance, deciding that the peculiar circumstances, with the long lapse of years, had extinguished, not only equitably, but legally, the authority of the husband.

The "Chirurgical Journal" of Leipsic -- a periodical of high authority and merit, which some American bookseller would do well to translate and republish, records in a late number a very distressing event of the character in question.

An officer of artillery, a man of gigantic stature and of robust health, being thrown from an unmanageable horse, received a very severe contusion upon the head, which rendered him insensible at once; the skull was slightly fractured, but no immediate danger was apprehended. Trepanning was accomplished successfully. He was bled, and many other of the ordinary means of relief were adopted. Gradually, however, he fell into a more and more hopeless state of stupor, and, finally, it was thought that he died.

The weather was warm, and he was buried with indecent haste in one of the public cemeteries. His funeral took place on Thursday. On the Sunday following, the grounds of the cemetery were, as usual, much thronged with visiters, and about noon an intense excitement was created by the declaration of a peasant that, while sitting upon the grave of the officer, he had distinctly felt a commotion of the earth, as if occasioned by some one struggling beneath. At first little attention was paid to the man's asseveration; but his evident terror, and the dogged obstinacy with which he persisted in his story, had at length their natural effect upon the crowd.

Spades were hurriedly procured, and the grave, which was shamefully shallow, was in a few minutes so far thrown open that the head of its occupant appeared. He was then seemingly dead; but he sat nearly erect within his coffin, the lid of which, in his furious struggles, he had partially uplifted.

He was forthwith conveyed to the nearest hospital, and there pronounced to be still living, although in an asphytic condition. After some hours he revived, recognized individuals of his acquaintance, and, in broken sentences spoke of his agonies in the grave.

From what he related, it was clear that he must have been conscious of life for more than an hour, while inhumed, before lapsing into insensibility. The grave was carelessly and loosely filled with an exceedingly porous soil; and thus some air was necessarily admitted. He heard the footsteps of the crowd overhead, and endeavored to make himself heard in turn. It was the tumult within the grounds of the cemetery, he said, which appeared to awaken him from a deep sleep, but no sooner was he awake than he became fully aware of the awful horrors of his position.

This patient, it is recorded, was doing well and seemed to be in a fair way of ultimate recovery, but fell a victim to the quackeries of medical experiment. The galvanic battery was applied, and he suddenly expired in one of those ecstatic paroxysms which, occasionally, it superinduces.

The mention of the galvanic battery, nevertheless, recalls to my memory a well known and very extraordinary case in point, where its action proved the means of restoring to animation a young attorney of London, who had been interred for two days. This occurred in 1831, and created, at the time, a very profound sensation wherever it was made the subject of converse.

The patient, Mr. Edward Stapleton, had died, apparently of typhus fever, accompanied with some anomalous symptoms which had excited the curiosity of his medical attendants. Upon his seeming decease, his friends were requested to sanction a post-mortem examination, but declined to permit it. As often happens, when such refusals are made, the practitioners resolved to disinter the body and dissect it at leisure, in private. Arrangements were easily effected with some of the numerous corps of body-snatchers, with which London abounds; and, upon the third night after the funeral, the supposed corpse was unearthed from a grave eight feet deep, and deposited in the opening chamber of one of the private hospitals.

An incision of some extent had been actually made in the abdomen, when the fresh and undecayed appearance of the subject suggested an application of the battery. One experiment succeeded another, and the customary effects supervened, with nothing to characterize them in any respect, except, upon one or two occasions, a more than ordinary degree of life-likeness in the convulsive action.

It grew late. The day was about to dawn; and it was thought expedient, at length, to proceed at once to the dissection. A student, however, was especially desirous of testing a theory of his own, and insisted upon applying the battery to one of the pectoral muscles. A rough gash was made, and a wire hastily brought in contact, when the patient, with a hurried but quite unconvulsive movement, arose from the table, stepped into the middle of the floor, gazed about him uneasily for a few seconds, and then -- spoke. What he said was unintelligible, but words were uttered; the syllabification was distinct. Having spoken, he fell heavily to the floor.

For some moments all were paralyzed with awe -- but the urgency of the case soon restored them their presence of mind. It was seen that Mr. Stapleton was alive, although in a swoon. Upon exhibition of ether he revived and was rapidly restored to health, and to the society of his friends -- from whom, however, all knowledge of his resuscitation was withheld, until a relapse was no longer to be apprehended. Their wonder -- their rapturous astonishment -- may be conceived.

The most thrilling peculiarity of this incident, nevertheless, is involved in what Mr. S. himself asserts. He declares that at no period was he altogether insensible -- that, dully and confusedly, he was aware of everything which happened to him, from the moment in which he was pronounced dead by his physicians, to that in which he fell swooning to the floor of the hospital. "I am alive," were the uncomprehended words which, upon recognizing the locality of the dissecting-room, he had endeavored, in his extremity, to utter.

It were an easy matter to multiply such histories as these -- but I forbear -- for, indeed, we have no need of such to establish the fact that premature interments occur. When we reflect how very rarely, from the nature of the case, we have it in our power to detect them, we must admit that they may frequently occur without our cognizance. Scarcely, in truth, is a graveyard ever encroached upon, for any purpose, to any great extent, that skeletons are not found in postures which suggest the most fearful of suspicions.

Fearful indeed the suspicion -- but more fearful the doom! It may be asserted, without hesitation, that no event is so terribly well adapted to inspire the supremeness of bodily and of mental distress, as is burial before death. The unendurable oppression of the lungs -- the stifling fumes from the damp earth -- the clinging to the death garments -- the rigid embrace of the narrow house -- the blackness of the absolute Night -- the silence like a sea that overwhelms -- the unseen but palpable presence of the Conqueror Worm -- these things, with the thoughts of the air and grass above, with memory of dear friends who would fly to save us if but informed of our fate, and with consciousness that of this fate they can never be informed -- that our hopeless portion is that of the really dead -- these considerations, I say, carry into the heart, which still palpitates, a degree of appalling and intolerable horror from which the most daring imagination must recoil. We know of nothing so agonizing upon Earth -- we can dream of nothing half so hideous in the realms of the nethermost Hell. And thus all narratives upon this topic have an interest profound; an interest, nevertheless, which, through the sacred awe of the topic itself, very properly and very peculiarly depends upon our conviction of the truth of the matter narrated. What I have now to tell is of my own actual knowledge -- of my own positive and personal experience.

For several years I had been subject to attacks of the singular disorder which physicians have agreed to term catalepsy, in default of a more definitive title. Although both the immediate and the predisposing causes, and even the actual diagnosis, of this disease are still mysterious, its obvious and apparent character is sufficiently well understood. Its variations seem to be chiefly of degree. Sometimes the patient lies, for a day only, or even for a shorter period, in a species of exaggerated lethargy. He is senseless and externally motionless; but the pulsation of the heart is still faintly perceptible; some traces of warmth remain; a slight color lingers within the centre of the cheek; and, upon application of a mirror to the lips, we can detect a torpid, unequal, and vacillating action of the lungs. Then again the duration of the trance is for weeks -- even for months; while the closest scrutiny, and the most rigorous medical tests, fail to establish any material distinction between the state of the sufferer and what we conceive of absolute death. Very usually he is saved from premature interment solely by the knowledge of his friends that he has been previously subject to catalepsy, by the consequent suspicion excited, and, above all, by the non-appearance of decay. The advances of the malady are, luckily, gradual. The first manifestations, although marked, are unequivocal. The fits grow successively more and more distinctive, and endure each for a longer term than the preceding. In this lies the principal security from inhumation. The unfortunate whose first attack should be of the extreme character which is occasionally seen, would almost inevitably be consigned alive to the tomb.

My own case differed in no important particular from those mentioned in medical books. Sometimes, without any apparent cause, I sank, little by little, into a condition of hemi-syncope, or half swoon; and, in this condition, without pain, without ability to stir, or, strictly speaking, to think, but with a dull lethargic consciousness of life and of the presence of those who surrounded my bed, I remained, until the crisis of the disease restored me, suddenly, to perfect sensation. At other times I was quickly and impetuously smitten. I grew sick, and numb, and chilly, and dizzy, and so fell prostrate at once. Then, for weeks, all was void, and black, and silent, and Nothing became the universe. Total annihilation could be no more. From these latter attacks I awoke, however, with a gradation slow in proportion to the suddenness of the seizure. Just as the day dawns to the friendless and houseless beggar who roams the streets throughout the long desolate winter night -- just so tardily -- just so wearily -- just so cheerily came back the light of the Soul to me.

Apart from the tendency to trance, however, my general health appeared to be good; nor could I perceive that it was at all affected by the one prevalent malady -- unless, indeed, an idiosyncrasy in my ordinary sleep may be looked upon as superinduced. Upon awaking from slumber, I could never gain, at once, thorough possession of my senses, and always remained, for many minutes, in much bewilderment and perplexity; -- the mental faculties in general, but the memory in especial, being in a condition of absolute abeyance.

In all that I endured there was no physical suffering but of moral distress an infinitude. My fancy grew charnel, I talked "of worms, of tombs, and epitaphs." I was lost in reveries of death, and the idea of premature burial held continual possession of my brain. The ghastly Danger to which I was subjected haunted me day and night. In the former, the torture of meditation was excessive -- in the latter, supreme. When the grim Darkness overspread the Earth, then, with every horror of thought, I shook -- shook as the quivering plumes upon the hearse. When Nature could endure wakefulness no longer, it was with a struggle that I consented to sleep -- for I shuddered to reflect that, upon awaking, I might find myself the tenant of a grave. And when, finally, I sank into slumber, it was only to rush at once into a world of phantasms, above which, with vast, sable, overshadowing wing, hovered, predominant, the one sepulchral Idea.

From the innumerable images of gloom which thus oppressed me in dreams, I select for record but a solitary vision. Methought I was immersed in a cataleptic trance of more than usual duration and profundity. Suddenly there came an icy hand upon my forehead, and an impatient, gibbering voice whispered the word "Arise!" within my ear.

I sat erect. The darkness was total. I could not see the figure of him who had aroused me. I could call to mind neither the period at which I had fallen into the trance, nor the locality in which I then lay. While I remained motionless, and busied in endeavors to collect my thought, the cold hand grasped me fiercely by the wrist, shaking it petulantly, while the gibbering voice said again:

"Arise! did I not bid thee arise?"

"And who," I demanded, "art thou?"

"I have no name in the regions which I inhabit," replied the voice, mournfully; "I was mortal, but am fiend. I was

merciless, but am pitiful. Thou dost feel that I shudder. --
My teeth chatter as I speak, yet it is not with the chilliness of
the night -- of the night without end. But this hideousness
is insufferable. How canst thou tranquilly sleep? I cannot rest
for the cry of these great agonies. These sights are more than
I can bear. Get thee up! Come with me into the outer Night,
and let me unfold to thee the graves. Is not this a spectacle
of woe? -- Behold!"

I looked; and the unseen figure, which still grasped me
by the wrist, had caused to be thrown open the graves of all
mankind, and from each issued the faint phosphoric radiance
of decay, so that I could see into the innermost recesses, and
there view the shrouded bodies in their sad and solemn
slumbers with the worm. But alas! the real sleepers were
fewer, by many millions, than those who slumbered not at all;
and there was a feeble struggling; and there was a general sad
unrest; and from out the depths of the countless pits there
came a melancholy rustling from the garments of the buried.
And of those who seemed tranquilly to repose, I saw that
a vast number had changed, in a greater or less degree, the
rigid and uneasy position in which they had originally been
entombed. And the voice again said to me as I gazed:

"Is it not -- oh! is it not a pitiful sight?" -- but, before
I could find words to reply, the figure had ceased to grasp
my wrist, the phosphoric lights expired, and the graves were
closed with a sudden violence, while from out them arose a

tumult of despairing cries, saying again: "Is it not -- O, God, is it not a very pitiful sight?"

Phantasies such as these, presenting themselves at night, extended their terrific influence far into my waking hours. My nerves became thoroughly unstrung, and I fell a prey to perpetual horror. I hesitated to ride, or to walk, or to indulge in any exercise that would carry me from home. In fact, I no longer dared trust myself out of the immediate presence of those who were aware of my proneness to catalepsy, lest, falling into one of my usual fits, I should be buried before my real condition could be ascertained. I doubted the care, the fidelity of my dearest friends. I dreaded that, in some trance of more than customary duration, they might be prevailed upon to regard me as irrecoverable. I even went so far as to fear that, as I occasioned much trouble, they might be glad to consider any very protracted attack as sufficient excuse for getting rid of me altogether. It was in vain they endeavored to reassure me by the most solemn promises. I exacted the most sacred oaths, that under no circumstances they would bury me until decomposition had so materially advanced as to render farther preservation impossible. And, even then, my mortal terrors would listen to no reason -- would accept no consolation. I entered into a series of elaborate precautions. Among other things, I had the family vault so remodelled as to admit of being readily opened from within. The slightest pressure upon a long lever that extended far into the tomb would cause the iron portal to fly back. There were arrangements also for the free admission of air and light, and convenient receptacles for food and water, within immediate reach of the coffin intended for my reception. This coffin was warmly and softly padded, and was provided with a lid, fashioned upon the principle of the vault-door, with the addition of springs so contrived that the feeblest movement of the body would be sufficient to set it at liberty. Besides all this, there was suspended from the roof of the tomb, a large bell, the rope of which, it was designed, should extend through a hole in the coffin, and so be fastened to one of the hands of the corpse. But, alas? what avails the vigilance against the Destiny of man? Not even these well-contrived securities sufficed to save from the uttermost agonies of living inhumation, a wretch to these agonies foredoomed!

There arrived an epoch -- as often before there had arrived -- in which I found myself emerging from total unconsciousness into the first feeble and indefinite sense of existence. Slowly -- with a tortoise gradation -- approached the faint gray dawn of the psychal day. A torpid uneasiness. An apathetic endurance of dull pain. No care -- no hope -- no effort. Then, after a long interval, a ringing in the ears; then, after a lapse still longer, a prickling or tingling sensation in the extremities; then a seemingly eternal period of pleasurable quiescence, during which the awakening feelings are struggling into thought; then a brief re-sinking into non-entity; then a sudden recovery. At length the slight quivering of an eyelid, and immediately thereupon, an electric shock of a terror, deadly and indefinite, which sends the blood in torrents from the temples to the heart. And now the first positive effort to think. And now the first endeavor to remember. And now a partial and evanescent success. And now the memory has so far regained its dominion, that, in some measure, I am cognizant of my state. I feel that I am not awaking from ordinary sleep. I recollect that I have been subject to catalepsy. And now, at last, as if by the rush of an ocean, my shuddering spirit is overwhelmed by the one grim Danger -- by the one spectral and ever-prevalent idea.

For some minutes after this fancy possessed me, I remained without motion. And why? I could not summon courage to move. I dared not make the effort which was to satisfy me of my fate -- and yet there was something at my heart which whispered me it was sure. Despair -- such as no other species of wretchedness ever calls into being -- despair alone urged me, after long irresolution, to uplift the heavy lids of my eyes. I uplifted them. It was dark -- all dark. I knew that the fit was over. I knew that the crisis of my disorder had long passed. I knew that I had now fully recovered the use of my visual faculties -- and yet it was dark -- all dark -- the intense and utter raylessness of the Night that endureth for evermore.

I endeavored to shriek-, and my lips and my parched tongue moved convulsively together in the attempt -- but no voice issued from the cavernous lungs, which oppressed as if by the weight of some incumbent mountain, gasped and palpitated, with the heart, at every elaborate and struggling inspiration.

The movement of the jaws, in this effort to cry aloud, showed me that they were bound up, as is usual with the dead. I felt, too, that I lay upon some hard substance, and by something similar my sides were, also, closely compressed. So far, I had not ventured to stir any of my limbs -- but now I violently threw up my arms, which had been lying at length, with the wrists crossed. They struck a solid wooden substance, which extended above my person at an elevation of not more than six inches from my face. I could no longer doubt that I reposed within a coffin at last.

And now, amid all my infinite miseries, came sweetly the cherub Hope -- for I thought of my precautions. I writhed, and made spasmodic exertions to force open the lid: it would not move. I felt my wrists for the bell-rope: it was not to be found. And now the Comforter fled for ever, and a still sterner Despair reigned triumphant; for I could not help perceiving the absence of the paddings which I had so carefully prepared -- and then, too, there came suddenly to my nostrils the strong peculiar odor of moist earth. The conclusion was irresistible. I was not within the vault. I had fallen into a trance while absent from home-while among strangers -- when, or how, I could not remember -- and it was they who had buried me as a dog -- nailed up in some common coffin -- and thrust deep, deep, and for ever, into some ordinary and nameless grave.

As this awful conviction forced itself, thus, into the innermost chambers of my soul, I once again struggled to cry aloud. And in this second endeavor I succeeded. A long, wild, and continuous shriek, or yell of agony, resounded through the realms of the subterranean Night.

"Hillo! hillo, there!" said a gruff voice, in reply.

"What the devil's the matter now!" said a second.

"Get out o' that!" said a third.

"What do you mean by yowling in that ere kind of style, like a cattymount?" said a fourth; and hereupon I was seized and shaken without ceremony, for several minutes, by a junto of very rough-looking individuals. They did not arouse me from my slumber -- for I was wide awake when I screamed -- but they restored me to the full possession of my memory.

This adventure occurred near Richmond, in Virginia. Accompanied by a friend, I had proceeded, upon a gunning expedition, some miles down the banks of the James River. Night approached, and we were overtaken by a storm. The cabin of a small sloop lying at anchor in the stream, and laden with garden mould, afforded us the only available shelter. We made the best of it, and passed the night on board. I slept in one of the only two berths in the vessel -- and the berths of a sloop of sixty or twenty tons need scarcely be described. That which I occupied had no bedding of any kind. Its extreme width was eighteen inches. The distance of its bottom from the deck overhead was precisely the same. I found it a matter of exceeding difficulty to squeeze myself in. Nevertheless, I slept soundly, and the whole of my vision -- for it was no dream, and no nightmare -- arose naturally from the circumstances of my position -- from my ordinary bias of thought -- and from the difficulty, to which I have alluded, of collecting my senses, and especially of regaining my memory, for a long time after awaking from slumber. The men who shook me were the crew of the sloop, and some laborers engaged to unload it. From the load itself came the earthly smell. The bandage about the jaws was a silk handkerchief in which I had bound up my head, in default of my customary nightcap.

The tortures endured, however, were indubitably quite equal for the time, to those of actual sepulture. They were fearfully -- they were inconceivably hideous; but out of Evil proceeded Good; for their very excess wrought in my spirit an inevitable revulsion. My soul acquired tone -- acquired temper. I went abroad. I took vigorous exercise. I breathed the free air of Heaven. I thought upon other subjects than Death. I discarded my medical books. "Buchan" I burned. I read no "Night Thoughts" -- no fustian about churchyards

-- no bugaboo tales -- such as this. In short, I became a new man, and lived a man's life. From that memorable night, I dismissed forever my charnel apprehensions, and with them vanished the cataleptic disorder, of which, perhaps, they had been less the consequence than the cause.

There are moments when, even to the sober eye of Reason, the world of our sad Humanity may assume the semblance of a Hell -- but the imagination of man is no Carathis, to explore with impunity its every cavern. Alas! the grim legion of sepulchral terrors cannot be regarded as altogether fanciful -- but, like the Demons in whose company Afrasiab made his voyage down the Oxus, they must sleep, or they will devour us -- they must be suffered to slumber, or we perish.

Printed in Great Britain
by Amazon